3"

Little Archie

Miles Gibson

Illustrated by Neal Layton

MACMILLAN CHILDREN'S BOOKS

First published 2004 by Macmillan Children's Books
a division of Macmillan Publishers Limited
20 New Wharf Road, London N1 9RR
Basingstoke and Oxford
www.panmacmillan.com

Associated companies throughout the world

ISBN 1 405 00278 6

1 3 5 7 9 8 6 4 2

A CIP catalogue record for this book is available from
the British Library.

Printed and bound in Great Britain by Mackays of Chatham plc, Kent

For Lisa,
who found him
M.G.

For Tiger Wilton
N.L.

Chapter 1

Archie lived with his mother and father
in a small house in the big city. He had
a goldfish and a baby brother. He called
the goldfish Bodger. The name of his
baby brother was Joe.

Archie led a regular life. He had regular meals and regularly cleaned his teeth, owned a regulation pencil box and regularly went to school.

"You have to stay regular," said his mother and father, who made a habit of giving people good advice.

Archie was as regular as clockwork.

 He was happy at home but he was even happier when he went to visit his Uncle Bernie.

Uncle Bernie had never lived a regular life. He lived in a house called the Jackdaw's Nest. He had a nose like a raspberry and whiskers sprouting from his ears. He lived with his books and his memories, a parrot and a gramophone. He also had a telescope and liked to sit on the roof at night to look at the moon and the stars. He counted the rings of Saturn and looked for signs of life on Mars.

Archie's mother and father disapproved of Uncle Bernie.

"He's a bad influence on the boy," they used to tell each other sadly. "He's barmy and he doesn't keep regular hours."

But Archie liked Uncle Bernie and enjoyed exploring the Jackdaw's Nest.

The rooms were crowded with cupboards and shelves. There were model boats and pictures of bears, potted plants and crocodile bones. There were

bottles of buttons and tins of paint and
dusty jars of boiled sweets. There were
plans for making rocket ships and recipes
for chocolate fudge and weather charts
of Africa and maps of mountains on
the moon.

Uncle Bernie would often lose one of his shoes in all this confusion and Archie would help him to search the house. The parrot would join them. Sometimes they would find the missing shoe and sometimes they would find something else, like a clockwork frog or a box of Bengal fireworks. The parrot enjoyed finding sultana biscuits.

After every visit to Uncle Bernie,
Archie would go home tired and dusty
and covered in cobwebs.

"It's not hygienic," his mother would
say, and shake her head and frown.

Chapter 2

The trouble began on Archie's birthday. It was a Saturday. Archie woke up at the regular time and went downstairs to open his presents. A birthday is an exciting event and Archie was hoping for surprises:

a conjuring set or a junior detective kit
containing interesting disguises.

But his mother gave him a fountain pen
and a large bottle of ink.

"You can write me a thank-you letter,"
she said. His mother liked
giving sensible presents.

Archie's father
gave him a racing
car, but the batteries
weren't included.

"You can always pretend," said his father, and went into the garden to look at his cabbages.

His baby brother gave him a smile and did a whoopsie into the potty.

Archie filled his new fountain pen and tried to pretend that the racing car worked, because people expect you to take an interest when you're having a birthday. But he felt a little disappointed.

It was late when Uncle Bernie arrived.

He brought Archie
a present wrapped in
a piece of blue waxed
paper and tied with a
length of hairy string.

"What is it?" said
Archie, and grinned.
He picked up the parcel and gave it
a squeeze. He knew it must be something
exciting. He gave it a sniff and held
it against his ear.

"Open it," said Uncle Bernie.

So Archie untied the string and discovered a small glass bottle filled with a yellow powder that glittered when he gave it a shake.

"It's Magic Shrinking Powder," Uncle Bernie said with a laugh. "I found it on my travels in China."

"Is it educational?" asked Archie's mother rather suspiciously.

"Is it suitable for a boy?" frowned his

father, holding the bottle against the light.

"What does it taste like?" said Archie.

"It's just for fun," Uncle Bernie warned
him. "You're not supposed to eat it!"
And he laughed again and shook Archie's
hand and then hurried back to the
Jackdaw's Nest to sit on the roof and
look at the stars.

Archie put the bottle on the shelf in his
bedroom. He crawled into bed and turned
out the light. But something strange was

happening. He could still see the bottle on the shelf. He blinked and rubbed his eyes. He thought he might have imagined it. He sat up and stared at the bottle. The Magic Shrinking Powder had started to glow in the dark. A soft, golden glow that seemed to fill the room with moonlight.

That's very strange, thought Archie, as he climbed out of bed. He stared at the shining powder for a long time. And then he thought, I wonder what it smells like?

So he took the bottle from the shelf, pulled out the cork and sniffed. It smelt of ginger biscuits, cherry cakes and macaroons.

Delicious, thought Archie. It smells delicious. And then, because it smelt so good, he forgot Uncle Bernie's warning. A taste can't do any harm, he said to himself.

He shook a little of the sparkling yellow powder into his hand and gave it a lick.

It fizzed and fizzled and frothed on
his tongue.

"Sherbet!" he grinned. And fell asleep.

Chapter 3

When Archie woke up the next morning he felt so peculiar that he knew something must be wrong. He was buried in blankets and smothered in sheets, as if the bed had grown around him.

It took several minutes to fight his way to the surface. He struggled from the bedclothes and climbed on to his pillow. That's not right, he thought. This pillow must have grown in the night. It's huge. It fills the room. It's utterly enormous. But when he looked at himself in the mirror he had the most terrible fright.

19

He was small. Very small. He had shrunk overnight. He was barely three inches tall.

"What are we going to do with him?" said his mother when she'd recovered from the shock. She placed him in a teacup for safety. "We can't send him to school – he doesn't fit his uniform."

"We could sell him to the circus," his father suggested hopefully.

"I don't think they do that sort of thing

any more," said his mother.

"Things must have changed since I was a boy," sighed his father.

"We should take him to Doctor Morris," said his mother.

So they put Archie in her handbag, because they were afraid of losing him, and carried him off to see the doctor.

The doctor peered at Archie and poked him with the end of a pencil. He frowned and scratched his head. He spent a long

time looking through the medical books
on his desk.

"It's impossible," said the doctor at last.
"It can't happen. And if it can't happen,
I can't treat him. Take him home and keep
him warm. Perhaps he will grow again."

"What happens if he doesn't grow?" demanded Archie's mother.

"You could always sell him to the circus," said the doctor.

They didn't take Archie home. They took him to the Jackdaw's Nest and gave him to Uncle Bernie.

Chapter 4

"Hello," said Uncle Bernie. "What's happened here?" He looked very excited.

He placed Archie on the parrot's perch and peered at him through a magnifying glass.

The parrot grumbled and ruffled his feathers. "I hope he doesn't want my banana," he said.

"This is *your* fault!" said Archie's father, wagging his finger at Uncle Bernie.

"You're a bad influence on the boy. Make him grow again."

"And don't send him back until he's normal," said Archie's mother.

Uncle Bernie promised to do his best.

"Don't worry," he told Archie as soon as his mother and father had gone. "I'm sure there's a bottle of Grow-More Powder around here somewhere. All we have to do is find it."

Together they began to search the house for the magic remedy. It wasn't easy for Archie because he was so small and had to be lifted on to the table to search through the jumble of bottles and boxes.

He found a dog whistle, a brass button and a box of peppermint balls. The parrot found a trumpet, a toothbrush and a Persian slipper. But they couldn't see anything that looked like a bottle of Grow-More Powder.

Uncle Bernie began to rummage through all the high cupboards and shelves in the room, but the dust was so thick that it tickled their throats and stung their noses.

"Stop it!" shrieked the parrot. "I'm

going to sneeze!" He closed his eyes
and shook his feathers. He snuffled and
shuffled and wheezed and finally gave
a great sneeze that shot Archie through
the open window!

29

Archie flew into the
sunshine with his arms
spread out like wings.
He turned a somersault
and kicked his legs.
He paddled his feet and
wriggled his hands. And, just when
he feared he might hit the ground, he
landed in the brim of a large lady's hat.

"Help!" shouted Archie.

"Help!" shouted the large lady.

A man came running and tried to soothe the large lady's nerves. "What happened?" he said.

"Something fell from the sky!" said the large lady, removing her hat and scowling into the fruit and feathers.

"It's a little bird!" said the man, pulling Archie from the hat and holding him gently in his hand. "My word, but he's an ugly little chap!"

"I'm not a bird," said Archie indignantly. "I'm a little boy!"

"Nonsense!" said the large lady. "Little boys don't fly. We'll take him to Mr Sprockett. He might have escaped from his pet shop."

Archie tried to explain what had happened, but it didn't make any difference, because when you're only three inches tall nobody listens to your opinions. So he found himself wrapped in the hat and taken to the pet shop on the corner of the street.

Mr Sprockett rubbed his nose and peered at Archie and shook his head.

"I've never seen anything like it," he said. "It's not a bird. I think it must be a rare sort of mouse. A very rare sort of mouse. It probably came from the zoo."

"I'm not a mouse!" said Archie. "I'm a little boy."

"Nonsense!" said the pet-shop owner impatiently. "Little boys don't nest in hats."

He placed Archie in a goldfish bowl with a slice of apple and a string of peanuts, and carried him to the zoo on the other side of the city.

But the head keeper stroked his moustache and closed one eye and said, "It's not a mouse. I think it's a small pink frog."

"I'm not a frog!" said Archie. "I'm a little boy."

"Nonsense!" said the head keeper. He didn't like to be contradicted. "Little boys don't come to the zoo in goldfish bowls. You're an undiscovered frog. You'll be famous. You'll probably appear on television." He dropped Archie into a green glass bottle with a twig and a caterpillar for company. "You'll have to go to the Natural History Museum in

America, where the professors will study you."

"I don't want to be studied," said Archie.

"I'm not going to argue with a frog!" said the head keeper indignantly. "I should be washing the elephants."

36

He marked the bottle Special Delivery
and told the assistant keeper to drive
down to the airport and put Archie on
the next plane to New York.

"Take care with this frog," the assistant
keeper told the captain. "He's the only
small pink frog of his kind."

Chapter 5

It was a long flight. When the plane
landed in America there was a limousine
with two security guards waiting to
collect the bottle and take it to the big
museum. The traffic was bad.

The weather was hot. When Archie arrived he was tired and angry. He sat on his twig and sulked. The caterpillar had fallen asleep and was dreaming of being a butterfly.

"I don't think it's a frog," declared the old museum professor as soon as Archie had been uncorked and placed in a saucer. "I believe it's a very intelligent mushroom."

"I'm not a mushroom!" said Archie.
"I'm a little boy."

"Nonsense!" said the old professor.
"Little boys aren't found in bottles."

"Mushrooms don't talk," argued Archie.

"That's why you're so special," said the
old professor. "We'll have to send you to
the Grand Academy in Japan. They take
a keen interest in mushrooms."

So the old professor dropped Archie into
a flowerpot filled with damp straw and

told the assistant professor to tell the
assistant professor's assistant to take it
to the airport.

"You've missed the plane to Japan,"
they told the assistant at the airport.

"But Captain Curly's airship is leaving this afternoon."

So they put Archie into the airship that was moored in a nearby field.

"Take good care of this mushroom," they told the captain. "He must be kept cool and dark."

It took a long time to reach Japan and

it was cold flying through the clouds because Archie had

to travel in the cargo basket with the suitcases and parcels. I must have been around the world, Archie thought. And I still haven't had my breakfast.

There was a helicopter waiting to take him to the Grand Academy. When Archie was unpacked he was placed in a glass tank in a room with Top Secret on the door.

"It's not a mushroom," said the men

at the Grand Academy. They wore rubber gloves and paper masks. They were very excited. They peered at him and scribbled in their notebooks. "It looks like a very small visitor from a distant galaxy in space." They started taking photographs.

"I'm not a distant visitor!" said Archie. "I'm a little boy."

"Nonsense!" said the president of the Grand Academy. "Little boys don't travel in flowerpots filled with straw."

He paused to comb his hair and have his photograph taken beside the tank. He asked if Archie had a message for the people of Earth.

"Yes," said Archie. "I missed my breakfast."

So they gave him a biscuit and watched him eat it.

"We'll have to send you to someone important who studies the moon and the stars," the president said at last.

"An astronomer," said the vice-president helpfully.

"An astronomer," said the president. And he placed Archie in a cardboard box marked High Security and sent him down to the harbour with a police escort to put him aboard an ocean liner.

"Take good care of this distant visitor," they told the captain. "He must not be disturbed."

Chapter 6

Archie spent a long time in the box. It was very dark and uncomfortable. When the sea was rough he was knocked and dropped and rolled and tumbled. And no one talked to him because the captain

had given instructions that he should
not be disturbed.

Finally the liner docked and Archie
managed to peek through one of the
ventilation holes in the box just in time
to find himself unloaded from the ship,
dropped into a satchel and
whisked away by motorbike.

The motorbike sped from
the harbour and took the
road to the big city.

49

I'm never going to escape, thought
Archie. I shall probably travel in circles
forever.

At that moment he felt himself lifted
from the satchel, dropped through a
letterbox and falling to the floor
with a thud.

The box broke open and Archie blinked.
He couldn't believe his eyes. He was
back in the Jackdaw's Nest!

"Hello," grinned Uncle Bernie when he
found Archie sitting on the floor.
"We'd thought we'd
lost you."

He was very pleased to see Archie.
He picked him up and took him into
the living room.

"Where have you been?" said the
parrot.

"Everywhere!" said Archie.

"I've found the Grow-More Powder.
It was hiding inside my winter slippers,"
said Uncle Bernie, and he held up a bottle
of sparkling green powder. He mixed a
little of the powder with water and

helped Archie sip it from a spoon.

"Does it work?" said Archie with a
frown. It tasted distinctly of gooseberries.

"I don't know," said Uncle Bernie.

At first nothing happened.

And then Archie felt a strange tickling
sensation in his fingers and a prickling
in his toes. He stretched and sprouted.
He creaked and gurgled. And slowly,
very slowly, Archie grew back to his
proper size.

"It works!" he said, and smiled.

Everyone seemed glad to see him again.
His mother cooked his favourite supper.
His father found batteries for the racing
car. His baby brother blew bubbles and

did a whoopsie into the potty.

"Regular as clockwork," said
his mother.

"We're back to normal," said his father.

Peculiar, thought Archie. A most
peculiar birthday. And then he yawned
and fell asleep.

The End